Also by .... Braccia:

Could it be That Way : Living with Autism

-   The story of how one man lived his life through childhood, education and career, eventually living a life influenced and consumed by autism.

Available via amazon.co.uk and amazon.com

See Michael's web site for more details:

http://michaelbraccia.wix.com/author-blog

Banfield Tales

A Collection of Short Stories

By Michael Braccia

A CIP catalogue record for this book
is available from the British Library

ISBN-13: 978-1517765958
ISBN-10: 1517765951

Enquiries via web site:

http://michaelbraccia.wix.com/author-blog

or email: michaelbraccia@hotmail.com

Some of the short stories portrayed in this book are partly based on true events. Many aspects of this portrayal have been fictionalised. The characters portrayed have also been fictionalised and any resemblance between them and actual living individuals should not be inferred.

To my wife, who continues to have limitless patience

Contents

Rocket Man in the King's Clothes   1

Killing Me Softly   9

Don't Take a Fence   23

Second Millennium   33

Young Love   43

Technical Kidnap   53

The Journey   63

The Birthday Present   69

Victor   81

Big Fish in a Small Pool   91

The Man in the Shed   105

Reunion for Ralph   115

Pigeon   123

Jenny of The Echo   131

She Blames Me   141

Introduction

Michael wrote most of the short stories in 2015 at the same time as producing his debut novel 'Could it be That Way : Living with Autism'. Some of them were entered into competitions including the famous Bridport Prize, but most were based on ideas that came to him when he least expected it. 'Killing Me Softly', surprisingly, was inspired by the music he was listening to at his local garage. Sitting in reception with his note book (it's never far away), he followed an idea he'd picked up from a book on creative writing. It was suggested that he write about the first thing he saw or heard in a particular situation. The Roberta Flack number 'Killing Me Softly' was drifting through the air into the garage reception. He completed a rough first draft by the time his car was ready.

There is an eclectic mix of short stories in this collection. One of the stories, 'Big Fish in a Small Pool' comes from the novel 'Could it be That Way'. Some stories are based on life in and around the fictional town of Banfield. Hopefully there is something for everyone, - quirky comic tales, romance, science fiction, family life, supernatural and ghost stories.

Because of the eclectic nature of the collection, you might like to read one story a day, or at least have a break between stories. Read the whole book in a day if you prefer, but a break might help to get the atmosphere and meaning of an individual story. Give you something to think about as you drive to work or wait for the bus or train.

Rocket Man in the King's Clothes

Darren wasn't brilliant on the acoustic guitar, but he enjoyed playing it now and then. He would find a song on Youtube or from his old vinyl collection, search for the chords and lyrics on the Web and try to create his own masterpiece (cover version). He had always considered what he would do if catapulted into the world of celebrity, but someone should have told him to be careful what he wished for.

Darren Cavannagh, a local lad, had done well in his chosen career of accountancy. Mind you, at the age of fifty-three he craved for something more. One Sunday morning, strumming along to various songs on YouTube, tucked away in the converted garage / 'recording studio', he came across an old favourite, Elton John's 'Rocket Man', one of the first vinyl singles he bought in the early seventies. At that time, post-lunar expeditions, there had been a number of space-orientated songs, notably Space Oddity (Bowie) and Rocket Man. Strange thing, after searching Google for the appropriate chords, he found the two songs to be remarkably similar; basically, the chords C, G, D7 and A9. Problem with Space Oddity though, there was one 'barred chord' and he couldn't play barred chords.

To the uninitiated, a barred chord is where you don't simply play a normal chord (three or four fingers spread over the first three frets of the guitar) but you play it lower down the neck of the guitar, maybe on the second or third fret (depending on the chord), with the forefinger holding down all six strings. He found this difficult. Also, playing Rocket Man, at first he just couldn't get the key right. It sounded nothing like the record. Fair enough, Elton played piano on the original version, so it would be different, but enough acoustic guitar covers existed on the web to tell Darren what it should sound like.

After much experimentation, Darren realised that instead of worrying about barred chords, he could get the 'key' right by placing the 'capo' (a metal device to hold down all six strings) just on the first fret. Bingo. The chords came to life and actually sounded like those cover versions. After four or five attempts playing Rocket Man he found the rhythm and managed a smooth change from chord to chord. Sounds good.

Let's get it spot on and film it, he thought. His basic digital camera wasn't 'David Bailey' but he could create a half-decent WMV file suitable for using in Movie Maker. First take – not bad. Second – couple of stumbles. Third – brilliant. That'll do. He didn't have a fantastic singing voice, but he captured the spirit of the original song (he thought so). I'll pop it on YouTube, he thought. I've already got an account.

The following day, amazingly, five people viewed the performance and two 'liked' it (modern social networking jargon, not meaning much to a fifty-three-year-old). Another day, fifteen people seemed to like it. A lull until the weekend. On Saturday another ten, and then... Wham.

During Sunday, two hundred people viewed the video and people started commenting on Twitter. In the office on Monday, most of the 'youngsters' (under thirty) had seen it. Some said they liked it, not just the internet 'like'. The following five days were the craziest of Darren's life. By Wednesday it had gone viral. Five thousand, then ten thousand hits. Comments on local radio, thirty thousand by Friday.

The following weekend, a mention on BBC Midlands News. 'Rocket Man sings in Banfield'. Fifty thousand. Fifty thousand hits. Word has it that Bernie Taupin, the man who wrote the original lyrics, had caught sight of the video. Where would all this lead?

Have you heard the story of the King's clothes? Hundreds of years ago, a slick salesman convinced the King in a land faraway that he could make him a suit of clothes so fine and so delicate, and so comfortable, that he would not be able to see them unless he was above-average intelligence. Only the smartest, noblest people could see the clothes. Of course, on the first fitting, the King was very impressed. He couldn't feel the clothes on his body, or see them, but he announced that they were 'the finest clothes in the land' and paid the man a handsome sum to complete the job. All the courtiers, clerks and various assistants were VERY impressed.

3

Oh, you are smart, Sir. Unfortunately, he was completely naked. It wasn't until a young boy walked past one day, and on seeing the very nude King, shouted 'The King is naked! He's altogether as naked as the day that he was born!' The King was ridiculed, and everyone else began to 'notice' that he was not, in fact, wearing any clothes. Hence the term the Kings Clothes Syndrome.

This is what Darren Cavannagh suffered from. He couldn't actually sing, and he was, in fact, useless at playing the guitar, but no one had the guts to tell him. Until now, and the declaration came from an unexpected source.

Laura Cavannagh is a straightforward sort of girl. What you see is what you get, no nonsense, tell it as it is. You get the drift. Blissfully unaware of Darren's escapades, she wasn't particularly impressed when he proudly announced the viral nature of his YouTube upload.

'They're laughing at you Darren.'

'No way, I'm a star.'

'You know your trouble, don't you?'

'What's that?'

'You're crap on the guitar and you don't sing in tune.'

'Oh.'

'Sorry love, but someone needed to say it.'

Darren's YouTube account was deleted by its owner before the night was out. No consolation for him receiving the message 'all your uploaded files will be deleted within 14 days.'

He wanted them gone. Pronto.

His loving wife had brought him down to earth. He had been wearing the King's Clothes.

Killing Me Softly

Susan Moore, an attractive girl, twenty-three, blond hair, lovely figure. She didn't have to 'dress to impress', but would readily catch the eye of a young man. However, she'd not been lucky with relationships and this tended to be the talk of the office for the other girls.

'Who is it tonight, Sue? The way you're going you'll be working your way through the partners.'

Inconceivable that any of the three senior partners at Cromer and Cromer, Solicitors, considered Susan to be a 'suitable partner' and, in any case, they were all married. Susan was of the same opinion.

'Don't be ridiculous. I prefer my men under thirty, thank you very much. Anyway, give it a rest, Jacqui, the last one wasn't too bad, you must admit.'

'Suppose, but they don't seem to last, do they? Anyway, are you off to the Lion again at lunchtime?'

'Not if you and Jenny are going.'

'Don't panic, we're back to the Crown Centre - getting new gear for the club on Saturday.'

'Just me then,' said Susan, relieved.

Simon was good-looking, fair-haired and well spoken. She'd seen him before at the Red Lion and desperately hoped he would notice her and make a move. Eventually he looked across and smiled. Every lunchtime the pub was the regular haunt of estate agents, solicitors, and secretaries like Susan Moore. On her own for once, usually accompanied by two of the girls from the office, Jacqui and Jenny, who never gave up. Today was a blessed relief. He walked over to her table.

'I'm Simon, what's your name?'

'Susan'

Almost slipping into "do you come here often" (for God's sake, she thought).

Within an hour of chatting, Roberta Flack playing on the jukebox in the background, not realising how quickly they seemed to be forming something; a bond, understanding, attraction. They agreed to meet the following night outside the Red Lion.

An exciting twenty-four hours for Susan, anticipating, hoping that this was the one. A previous succession of boyfriends only yielded frustration and hurt.

She met Mark at a friend's 21st birthday party. He seemed keen, but she soon realised that his eye had a tendency to rove on a far too regular basis. At the age of twenty she liked to have fun, and although not yet ready to settle down, she had a preference for loyalty and stability. Mark would never provide that.

Roger, on the other hand, buried his head in books. Susan spent three months helping him revise for his Law finals. Yes, he may well have made perfect husband material, and maybe Susan is never going to be totally satisfied. She was ashamed to admit she simply found him boring.

Keith was another matter. Certainly not the student type, a local mechanic, he had chatted her up when her car went in for service. This one turned out to be a disaster, always recovering from the last binge with his mates, who were constantly on the scene.

She'd like to settle down one day. Marriage, kids, the lot. Why not with Simon? Susan, she told herself, take your time.

She arrived outside the pub, right next to the alleyway. She'd never been down there, and just as she was wondering whether he would turn up (she had been let down a few times recently), someone called her name. She spun round to see a man turn into the alleyway - Simon, obviously. She followed him and quickly realised how dark it was down there. Feeling that she was in a low-budget B-movie, she smiled to herself while at the same time sensing a contradiction. Nervous, even slightly scared, and could almost hear the eerie movie soundtrack, but could smell the dampness of the alley. But this was no film script. A chink of light further down the passageway illuminated only her hands. Footsteps, coming closer, someone breathing hard. Then, she was suddenly knocked over. He was pulling at her clothes, on top of her immediately. He struck her hard across the face. She was dazed, but aware.

The rape was over in minutes. She knew the man had worn a mask, and he was gone.

Violated, shocked, angry, ashamed. She straightened her clothes. No blood, she thought, but there would be a bruise she would have to explain, already developing on her left cheek.

For some crazy reason she decided that she would deal with this herself. No police. Her six years as a secretary at Cromer and Cromer had taught her that victims of sexual assault are often not dealt with as they should be and convictions are not always easy.

Just six months ago, a young girl had been assaulted in the town. There was pretty convincing evidence, a retracted confession, and the accused had previous convictions. The defence barrister tore her to pieces on the witness stand. Susan was in court that day, and she will never forget the look of sheer desperation on the girl's face.

He went down for aggravated assault, probably released after a year or so with good behaviour, but the press were not kind to the girl.

'Led him on,' they said.

'She had it coming, dressed like that.'

Maybe it's changing, but she instinctively knew that she must deal with this herself; and she was convinced it was Simon. Otherwise, where was he now? He had given Susan his address - Flat 23, Smith Court, Cheslet Road – she would confront him. If, at close quarters, she was then 100% sure he was the one, she would kill him.

Susan drove back to the house she shared with two students. She hardly ever saw them. Tonight was no exception; just as well considering the bruise that was quickly developing on her cheek. She needed to get in the shower and try to wash away the horrible, filthy feelings that swirled round both her mind and body.

After showering, she dressed, slowly, somehow managing to stay calm. She took a knife from the kitchen, no one about she thought, and placed it carefully in her bag.

She sat for a while in her room, thinking, knowing what she had to do. She put the radio on for a welcome distraction. 'Killing me softly'. Ironic that should be playing. Could it be that easy. She intended to kill him that night, but she still had doubts. Since the day of the attack, only the man's mask separated her from being completely sure of his identity. If she was wrong, God, just the thought.

Back in her car, Susan found herself driving to Cheslet Road, as if on auto-pilot; and although she knew Cheslet Road quite well, this would be the first time she'd been to Simon's flat.

Arriving at the flat changed everything, absolutely everything. As she walked through the open door, there was no doubt that Simon was dead, stabbed through the chest, blood everywhere. No immediate emotion. Why should she care anyway after what he did, but had it really been him? Had he done it before to someone else and they wreaked the revenge she now sought?

Leave now, phone the police, get out now.

She was in the street before she made up her mind. Instinct kicked in, she hadn't touched anything.

The door already open when she arrived. She had intended to confront him and use the knife hidden in her bag, but someone had beaten her to it. Her hands shaking as she fumbled with her car keys. That was when she saw him, leaving the building with a single glance in her direction. Did she recognise him? Did he know Simon? Not sure, but she had to get away.

Susan drove back to the house as fast as she could, expecting to be followed. Who is that, is he the killer, why Simon? Does he know about the attack on me? All these and many other thoughts surged through her mind. She had met someone, been assaulted, violated, intended to confront him, found him dead, then this man, this strange man, leaving the block of flats after Susan had found Simon's body. Something familiar about him. However, she decided not to contact the police.

Two weeks passed and nothing happened. Absolutely nothing. Susan scoured the local papers, radio, TV News. Nothing. How can this be? Wouldn't Simon be missed? That was when the phone calls started.

'I know what you did.'

'Who are you? What am I supposed to have done?'

'Simon didn't deserve that.'

'I've done nothing. Please, who are you? What's going on?'

'You will be punished.'

Susan considered going to the police, but she had left it so long, and struggled to think what she would say to them.   Maybe a foolish decision, but she grabbed her keys, went down to the car and once again drove to the flat. She pulled up outside, somehow expecting to see the same man there, or maybe even Simon, although she knew that was impossible. Walking carefully up the stairs towards Simon's flat she had a feeling of dread. Arriving at the door, there was no police tape and the name on the door plate read 'James Haslett'. She was certain that it read 'Simon Edridge' that night, the night she had found him dead. What the hell was going on?

Again, she left the block of flats and returned home; unsure what to do and not knowing what was going to happen next.

The following day, more calls; more of the same.

'I know what you did. Girls like you are all the same.'

'Who the hell are you?'

Phone down.

The phone calls continued, every day for over three weeks, and then gradually became less frequent. One occasion, however, really spooked her. She had relaxed a little, not having received a call for over a week. Picking up the phone at first there was no voice, but she could hear faint music. It gradually got louder as the man spoke.

'You cause your own problems, girls like you.'

Music getting louder. She recognised it, reminding her of that night.

'Not long now.'

She then heard nothing and another two weeks passed, but she could not forget Simon, or the horrible things that had happened to her. They refused to leave her mind.

She somehow plucked up courage to speak to the 'new' occupant of flat 23, James Haslett. Again, that same feeling of dread on the stairs, the hairs on the back of her neck standing up. She knocked the door, twice. Haslett slowly opened the door, greeting Susan with a smile. That feeling again. Something familiar about...

'Drink?'

'Oh, thanks, I'm driving - lemon and lime please.'

'Sensible girl.'

'Don't take chances.'

He poured the drinks and sat opposite her.

'I've got some old vinyl singles from the seventies. Would you like to hear some?'

'Yeh, love nostalgia.'

This isn't Simon, but he's so familiar. Even his smell, the same after-shave, his mannerisms. So familiar. The arm carrying the stylus slowly creaked into place. Spinning at 45rpm the record received the stylus and the music started. As Roberta Flack started to sing, James turned round to face Susan, taking off his red-rimmed glasses. Susan couldn't help it, she had to challenge him.

'It's you – you were outside the flat that night. Who are you?'

Susan sensed she was in trouble.

'My good-looking brother always gets the girls. I have to fight for mine. We both inherited a share of our parents' fortune when they were killed in a car accident ten years ago. We have no need to go to work but we both like female company. The flat's in Simon's name, or at least it was. I changed mine to Haslett after the accident. You might say it affected me in a number of ways. You know what Susan; I've really missed you since our meeting in the alleyway. Just in case you wondered, yes, the front door is locked.'

He turned the volume up once more. Susan was not at work the following morning. Killing me softly with his song...

Don't Take a Fence

Four hours I've been here. Four long, arduous hours. I've now used half a tub of Fenceguard (other fence products are also available) painting my flippin' fences. I feel tired, angry, stupid, and most of all embarrassed. Why? Let me tell you what happened.

It all started really well on a lovely day in June last year. I'd got the day off and Anita had given me her usual list of jobs I needed to complete; main one - the fences at the side of the house. So you can understand the layout of our grand estate (that is, 3-bedroomed linked-detached). I will explain. As you look at the front of the house, the garage is to the right ('linked' to the neighbour's house next door), the front door and porch is in the middle, and to the left is the side entrance to the garden. Further to the left (try to picture this in your mind) is the bottom of each of the gardens attached to the houses in the next street, which is at right-angles to our street. Hope that makes sense. Anyway, these are the fences crying out for a new coat of Fenceguard. Also, at the front of the entrance (before I carried out my maintenance duties, and by the way, we call it the tradesmen's entrance) was a very rusty metal gate. When we first moved in we could hear knocking and clanking in the night. I'm sure Anita is wrong when she says I've quoted Benny Hill's song too many times: 'was it the trees-a-rustling or the hinges of the gate, or Ernie's ghostly gold tops a-rattling in their crates'. She's probably right. She's also right when she says I need a new script writer.

So, two jobs regarding the front gate - rub it down to the bare metal and paint it (black, says Anita). We'll padlock it and put a 'stopper' at the back of the gate to prevent it from clanking. Stopper is my technical term for a house-brick.

Now, for security reasons, that is, when we first moved in, to stop our hyperactive six-year-old from escaping (possibly climbing the metal gate) we had a proper man in who fitted a robust wooden gate half-way down the side passageway. Hope this makes sense. So, picture the scene, a new-ish wooden gate to which we added bolts that cannot be reached from the outside. This is where my problem started.

On the fateful day, I moved all my tools, tub of Fenceguard, sandpaper and black metallic paint and brushes into the passageway, between the two gates. I used Fenceguard for the wooden gate and started to 'fenceguard' the three side fences (bottom of the garden for the neighbours to the left). Anita called me, suggesting a break. I left the metal gate unlocked, walked round the back of the house, bolting the wooden gate, nice and secure, nice and snug, and went in the house via the backdoor.

Sandwich, cake, nice cuppa and one hour later, this is where I made my big mistake. For some reason only known to the Gods, and I will never be able to explain it, I carried all the other stuff I needed (towel, rags for wiping off excess paint and so on) through the house, out the front door, and into the side passageway. It's now about one o'clock and Anita calls out:

'Going to see Mom, see you at tea-time.'

'Ok love; send my best to your Mom.'

I love my mother-in-law to bits, but I'd rather be rubbing down and painting a metal gate, thank you very much.

It took about half an hour to finish rubbing down the gate, and maybe about the same to paint it. I carefully closed the gate, padlocked it and placed the brick to stop the clanking. Shall we call it the anti-clanking brick? Anyway, I am now in the passageway, locked outer gate, and if you remember, locked inner gate. Trapped like a dog. Correction, a dog would have had more sense.

Think now, think, you berk. You hurt your back a couple of weeks ago just cleaning the car; you can't climb either of the gates, or the fences. Anita's gone to her Mom's, John's with his Auntie til about seven. Flippin' Eck, what next? It was at this stage I had my first (or should I say second) stupid moment. One of my neighbours walked by and waved.

'Hi David, keeping busy?'

'Yeh, these fences take some painting.'

'Want a hand?'

'No, it's keeping me out of mischief; thanks anyway.'

Little did they know I was the Prisoner of Askaban, Bird Man of Alcatrass, and Prat of Banfield. Good grief, why don't they just bugger off.

'Sure you're ok?'

'Course, see you later.'

You will, of course, believe me when I say that each and every neighbour we have got to know over the five years living at the house naturally decided to walk past, each one looking in my direction, acknowledging me. I hadn't seen some of these people for weeks. The Gods are, indeed, cruel.

2.00 p.m.

Right, I'll have to do something. I am too embarrassed to call for help. No way am I telling Mike or Joan next door that I'm trapped, whether it's like a dog or otherwise. I'll never hear the end of it. Reminds me, while I seemed to have plenty of time on my hands; last Christmas was interesting. I went round Mike and Joan's to wish them 'Merry Christmas' and Mike offered me a whisky. It was about 9.00 p.m., and I simply wanted to say thank you for our presents and pass a book to Mike about Egypt that I know he'd enjoy. Could do with it now. Good at tunnelling, the Egyptians.

I told Anita I'd be about 30 minutes. Well, at around 11.30 p.m. (Joan had gone to bed), and half a dozen whiskies later, Mike helped me out of the front door. Now, if you've followed the geography lesson so far, you will know that I needed to turn right to go home. It's not far. I turned left, staggered into another driveway and sat down, quite dizzy. Mike was brilliant. He half-carried me back home. Now, you see, I don't really remember all the details. Mike filled in the gaps at a later date as he can take his drink better than me. Mike, bless him, has embellished the story as the months have fluttered by. Anyway, he told everyone, and I've been asked about my drinking habits quite frequently since, and been offered maps and a loan of a Sat Nav. As you will now appreciate, I don't need another story to do the rounds.

Back to the plot.

It's now 3.00 p.m., and I've exhausted all the tidying up and double-checking the metallic paint. I'll paint a fence again. It's got to be dry and ready for another coat. Good idea, Dad always says I should give it two coats. Thanks Dad. I think I'm going mad as I suddenly remember the joke he told me about the man who stole a garden gate and asked for 23 other fences to be taken into consideration. Told you.

'Hi David.'

This time it's Jack from the other side (no, I mean the other side of the fence - not that sort of story, so not in the spiritual sense).

'Hiya Jack, you ok?'

'What you up to?'

'You know, giving them an extra coat.'

'You seem a bit wound up, sure you're ok?'

'Fine, just keeping myself busy. Beats going to visit the outlaws.'

(Go away Jack, you're a great bloke, but I don't need this right now).

'Know what you mean. Anyway, if you need any help, give me a shout.'

Giving someone 'a shout' was the initial plan, but that had been instantly shelved due to the embarrassment factor. If only he knew. Now I'm feeling stupid, really stupid, and extremely embarrassed. I think you could fry an egg on my face.

5.30 p.m.

Surely she'll be back soon. I've sat down and stood up so many times when people have walked past I feel like a jack-in-the-box on some performance enhancing drug; and I'm bursting for a pee. This could be interesting if Anita's not back soon.

5.50 p.m.

I will always remember that time. My darling wife returns. I have never been so glad to see her. Unfortunately, I don't greet her quite as I should, and I'm lucky she didn't leave me there.

'For God's sake, how long do you need for a chat with your Mom?'

'What's up with you?'

'Nothing. Just get round the back, quick, and open the gate.'

'What's happened?'

'Just do it, Anita, please.'

Anita is sworn to secrecy, but I'm sure that some of our friends and neighbours know something. How silly for a grown man to be too embarrassed to shout for help.

'I would have climbed the fence', they might say.

'Why didn't you shout up as we walked past?'

They didn't actually say anything, Anita is forgiven, and I always, always keep at least one of the gates unlocked when I work at the side of the house.

Thanks for listening.

Second Millennium

Leo Banks works for iCloud Systems, one of the corporations that ordinary people have not heard of, but they are involved in the lives of every one of us. Everything about us is stored in the 'cloud', a collection of data on every conceivable topic - health records, savings, mortgage, employment history, criminal convictions – for every registered person on the planet. The year 2039 has seen an increase in 'non-registered persons' and the authorities do everything in their power to pull them back into the system. People who do not use a computer or are not connected to the internet think they are immune, but they are wrong. We all have a number, we are being monitored, and we are all stored on the cloud. Since the early part of the 21st Century, more and more computer programs and personal data have been uploaded to the Cloud. Some people continue to use the old technology hard disks (possibly just for backups) but most of us have become more confident and trusting in the cloud-based storage of our data.

The Cloud itself is run by a number of corporations, subsidised by the five major world nations - USA, The Russian Federation, China, Africa and the European Union. Britain has long been subsumed by the EU, and is now one of the main bases for the physical location of the cloud servers. The servers themselves are essentially storage systems for vast amounts of data. Back in 2015, when Leo was still at school, everyone still used hard disks and USB memory sticks. Things have changed. Personal data is accessed through a device worn on your wrist which also encompasses a watch and communication device. The data is simultaneously stored in the Cloud.

Saturday 31st December 2039. Thirty-four years old, Leo has recently been appointed as Senior Analyst at iCloud Systems. Today is his big test. He is supervising a team of engineers who are preparing for what is now known as the 'Second Millennium'. The last time the world panicked about a date was on 31st December 1999. At the time it was feared that planes would fall out of the sky and hospitals would close. None of that happened, but back then we lived in a different era. Five years ago, the USA placed nuclear missiles in orbit to control China and The Russian Federation; co-members of the Committee, but still their sworn enemies. Everything is computer controlled. One password from the President could trigger Armageddon. To ensure that doesn't happen, the date they are planning for is 31st December 2040. Exactly one year to go.

Leo has other concerns. The servers they installed create a lot of heat. Even these days, computer experts are constrained by the laws of physics. Electronic circuits and processor chips still get hot and they have to be cooled. The data centres in which they are securely stored present a massive fire risk -

vulnerable to terrorism, but also natural occurrences of fire when cooling systems fail. Leo has employed the services of a company providing a 'failsafe' method of preventing fires in data centres. This involves a two-minute warning to all staff to vacate the main server rooms and then the IGFSS system is triggered (Inert Gas Fire Suppression System). It sounds a frightening prospect. When the system is activated, the system pumps argon, nitrogen and carbon dioxide into each server room. This reduces the oxygen level to below 15%. By reducing the oxygen to this level it will suppress a fire. This would not be sufficient to maintain life within an oxygen depleted environment. The IGFSS discharges the payload of gases within two minutes of a fire alarm.

With his team, Leo completed the tests, and they were reasonably confident that the 'Second Millennium' would pass without problems. There was, however, no guarantee. He continued, with no evidence, to harbour private concerns and lingering doubts about the upcoming event. Leo was unable to voice these concerns at senior management meetings, held in New York every three months. He would be ridiculed as it was just a feeling. These days, everything worked through logic, not emotion or instinct.

Sunday 30th December 2040.

Leo spent the day with his wife, Katie, in their lodge in Ashbourne, Derbyshire. The main Data Centre was located in a small village called Fenny Bentley on the Buxton Road, considered to be pretty much in the centre of the country, easier to defend and without the ravages of the enormous coastal tides that Britain's beaches and sea-walls endured today.

'Are you ready for tomorrow?' concern showing in her voice.

'As ready as we'll ever be.'

'Why are you going in tonight?'

'There are a few things I need to check. Don't forget, we've got eighty people working in the local data centre. At least thirty-five of them are vulnerable if the gas failsafe systems don't work.'

'Let me know if you need anything, and please be careful.'

Leo worked until the early hours of the morning, and couldn't find any issues to prove his theory. Everything seemed to be in place. After a short sleep back at the lodge, he ate breakfast and once again made his way to the Data Centre. Again, his instinct told him that something was wrong. They had missed something. The Second Millennium will trigger a program bug causing untold problems, and he would be in a server room, on shift, between 9.00 p.m. on New Year's Eve through to 6.00 a.m. on 1st January. He had to get out of there by midnight. He just had to. On the one hand he felt honour bound to warn his colleagues so they could get to safety as well, but if he was wrong and everything went smoothly after he had made a fuss it might cost him his job. If he was right however...

Leo and Katie were unable to have children. They only had each other. She was his whole life. If he was right about the Second Millennium 'bug', his visions of a whole team of analysts being trapped in server rooms with the oxygen being sucked out, doors locked, all exits sealed - effectively, execution chambers become reality. If that were to be the case, anything could happen. The missile systems might also be triggered. He had seen the system diagrams, but could not describe to his superiors the technical reason why he considered them so vulnerable. He felt so selfish, but he knew what he had to do. To avoid attracting attention to himself, he would make some sort of excuse around 11.00 p.m. Migraine, perhaps, or make out he'd forgotten something from home.

Enough time to leave the centre, ten minutes to get home, collect Katie and make their way to the bunker. All personnel from grade six and above (he was grade eight) had electronic keys for the bunker in Ashbourne. Located in an innocuous building in

Windmill Lane off the Buxton Road, barely five minutes from their lodge. Two hundred feet below the surface, food and water for up to six months. Could it really happen? One stage at a time. Who else should he tell - he might be wrong, and he certainly didn't want a mass panic.

10.30 p.m.

Christ, he thought, I can't stand this. I can't afford to take a chance. I'll get Katie and we'll be safe. He felt so sorry for those he would leave behind. If he could think of a way of warning them at the last minute, he'd do it. He thought about his father, Mike, who had worked in I.T. for twenty-five years. Mike never experienced anything like this, but Leo would have benefited from his knowledge and calm manner. He had lost him just over two years ago, Christmas 2038, and he still missed him terribly. It was just him and Katie now. 11.05 p.m.

'Ted, I've got to pop home for those analysis sheets. I won't be long.'

'You don't want to miss the fun, Leo. I'll get the coffee on ready for later.'

Leo arrived back at the lodge. Forty minutes to get Katie into the car and over to the bunker and safety. He'd already packed a bag for each of them. He would give her ten minutes to gather some personal items.

'Is it happening, just as you said?'

'I still don't know. I honestly don't know, but we can't afford to take the chance.'

'Just need my bag, make-up, some bits and pieces.'

They drove slowly away from the lodge, their home for the last six months. It would take less than ten minutes to reach the secure site, a disused farm on Windmill Lane. After two turnings, he became aware that they were being followed, but he said nothing. I've got time, he thought, to double-back and make sure. He turned round in a lay-by, making his way back into central Ashbourne. Yes, they were following. He turned at the next island, back towards the bunker. Twenty minutes, still time. Just a mile from the site, on the deserted lane. Katie suddenly spoke. She sounded different.

'Stop the car, Leo.'

'What?'

'Just stop the car.'

As he pulled over, the other car also stopped. Two men got out and walked towards them. Katie took the car keys as one of the men opened Leo's door, beckoning him to get out. Katie moved over into the driver's seat. Leo was ushered into the back seat of the other car.

'We are aware that you have some concerns, but they are unfounded. You personally signed off the tests last year.'

'Who are you?'

'Let's just say we represent the interests of iCloud Systems.'

They continued to question him, as Katie drove away. She's betrayed me.

Midnight. A signal from his communicator.

'Leo, its Ted. God, the doors are locked. There's nothing we can do. The...'

Then, nothing. He had been right all along. Time would only tell if the world would survive the Second Millennium.

Young Love

She arrived late for the interview. Mr Lord, Menswear Manager, already becoming impatient. Not a man to keep waiting.

'If she's not here in ten minutes, tell her to forget it' he said to the Assistant Manager, Rose, used to his ways, but knew that he'd give anyone a chance.

Just in time for me. I was tidying up the racks of trousers left bedraggled by a stream of clumsy customers. If they pick up a pair to inspect, they should really make the effort. Fourteen years old, two hours a day after school in the Co-op MensWear department. Good money. I even managed to cram in some French vocab revision behind the counter while Mr Lord attended a meeting. No customers in the shop. Rose said it's ok as long as there's nothing else to do and Mr Lord's not around.

Very often it was quiet in those last two hours of the day. I managed to cram in twenty minutes homework most days, and did the rest at home.

The girl appeared in our lives and I was distracted to an extent I was too young to understand. Not that she was particularly beautiful (in the way I thought the dancers on Top of the Pops were beautiful). Older than me certainly, and pretty, but there was something. Rose noticed my reaction.

'Steady on David; you've mixed the 32 long with the 38 short. Seems you've lost concentration.'

'Sorry Rose.'

She could never be late for me. I didn't say to myself 'I'm in love' nor did any specific coherent thoughts come to mind. I'd only heard about love at first sight in films. She just was. She was there. Thankfully, she got the job, three days a week while studying to be a nurse. Sixteen. I'd fallen for someone two years older than me. Sure, I'd fancied girls at junior school and at the Friday night disco that Banfield Grammar shared with the Banfield Girls' High. Bit of a cattle market really. Even at that age, I cringed at the cliché-ridden approaches we all made, mostly refused. Did we really want to dance anyway?

Her name was Anne. Curly, mousy hair falling over her eyes. Something about that cheeky smile, dimpled cheeks. Others seeing past my gaze might have said she was slightly overweight. For me, she was perfect. She smiled when she first saw me and her lips mouthed 'hello'. An instant connection. She giggled as I dropped a pair of 36 medium when she arrived, late, for her interview. I realised afterwards that she would always be late. I liked that. We worked together for over a year at the shop and she always breezed in, ten minutes after everyone else; her face flushed, green eyes gleaming, tousled hair. Sometimes I could hardly stand it. I just wanted to hold her, love her.

We began by claiming the same two seats in the canteen. Sometimes we had the place to ourselves. Rose didn't encourage what she called 'fraternisation' among the staff, but she saw no harm in us having our break at the same time. Looking back, we were more like brother and sister, pals, whatever the expression might be. We'd talk about anything, except us, usually.

One conversation stopped me in my tracks. She had a boyfriend. Peter was nineteen, and his sister Kate worked in another department at the shop. Kate had helped Anne to get the interview. I longed for her to say that Peter was not right for her. She was certainly irritated by his lack of attention, always working, training to be a plumber. He came in once, very smooth, so old. I felt so small, so inadequate, so young. I couldn't say she was 'my girl' but I told myself that if there was any justice in the world, she would be. Peter was wrong for her.

Every night at 6.00 p.m. I walked her to the bus station in Banfield, about a mile from the shop. Her bus took her in the opposite direction to where I lived, out of town about five miles. I wanted to hold her hand, caress her shoulder, but we just walked. I knew she liked me. Night after night, I asked her if she would be free to go to the Friday night disco (we could invite guests), the pictures, or maybe a walk in the country. Every night the same excuses; I knew it was about Peter, maybe me as well - too young, and she probably didn't like me quite enough, but I kept hoping. I thought about her all the time. Nights were the worst. Going over in my mind what to say to her, anything that might make a difference.

A glimmer of hope. One day, Anne wasn't at work when I arrived at 4.00 p.m. Kate took me to one side.

'Peter's dumped her.'

'Is she ok?'

'Bit upset. She's got nursing exams this week as well.'

I tried not to feel pleased, as I wanted her to be happy, even if it wasn't with me. She was there the next day.

'Hi'

'You ok? Heard about Peter.'

'We'll talk later - bus station cafe?'

How I got through the next two hours I just don't know. My head was spinning, and I ached. Please give me a chance, I thought.

'That walk in the country. Still on?'

'Course. It's half-term next week. Can you get a day off?'

'Let you know tomorrow.'

She had never let me kiss her, and in some ways it didn't matter. I just wanted to be with her. When we met at the bus station the following Wednesday, armed with food and drink for the day, I don't think I'd ever been happier. We decided to walk to a country park about four miles south of Banfield, Himley Hall. Chance to talk. She seemed to open up and let me into her world. Still no touching, no kisses, but at that moment she was mine.

We arrived at Himley Hall, watched the sailing boats and ducks on the lake, families queuing up for pitch and putt. Plenty of space to find a spot for a picnic. Under a huge, ancient oak by the side of the lake, towering over us, protective. She laid out a blanket and we both sat, opening our sandwich boxes for an early lunch. We finished, and she lay down, putting her lead on my lap. She let me stroke her hair.

'That's nice, David.'

'Are you happy?'

'This is lovely. I feel safe with you.'

47

She dozed in the sun. I could feel the soft skin of her cheeks on my fingers, and she sighed as I caressed her hair.

'Be nice if we could stay here forever,' she said.

'You know how I feel about you Anne.'

'Don't spoil it. Enjoy it. Just as we are.'

'Do you like me?'

'Course I do, but don't rush it.'

I was too young to know how to handle what was happening to me. If it is possible to understand love at that age, I loved her with every fibre. For now, she was mine; bubbly, giggly and funny. We walked to the edge of the Hall grounds, climbing over a hedge. Best adventure I'd ever had, the field deserted, until Anne screamed.

'Bull !!'

I thought she was joking, but there it was. We had ventured into farmland, and although we couldn't stop laughing, it was frightening too. Danger over, as I helped her back over the hedge, she slipped and fell against me. She brought her lips to mine. We kissed for what seemed like hours and she held me tight, knowing what to do and what to avoid. No more than a kiss, but tender, unforgettable. We lay down, holding hands. She smiled, stroking my hair.

'I do like you. I think of you as my best friend.'

'Just friends?'

'We'll see. Kiss me again.'

I didn't see Anne at work until the following week. She had finished her exams, but seemed pre-occupied. Silence followed us, stalked us, on our way to the bus station. She gave me a peck on the cheek before getting on the bus.

'See you...'

I was confused, but she had kissed me. Don't think I'd done anything wrong. Next day, she wasn't at work. Kate asked me to see her in the canteen.

'Anne's left. She wanted me to tell you.'

'What's going on?'

'David, I'm really sorry. She's been offered a job at a hospital in Birmingham. Full time, training, college, the lot.'

'You know we went out together. Why should a job make a difference?'

'David... she's back with Peter.'

If Kate had hit me with a mallet she couldn't have delivered a more crushing blow. She's back with Peter. Was that a goodbye kiss at the bus station? Only ten days ago we were so happy.

'David, you've got to understand. She's got a life ahead of her – career, everything. She really liked you...likes you, but its best this way. Try to forget her.'

Forget her...

Technical Kidnap

Banfield Grammar was always ahead of its time. Security is important to every school in the country, but Banfield really went for it. However, there's always a price to pay, quite apart from the financial cost. You could also argue they were the victims of their own success in the sense that some of the pupils were too clever for their own good, particularly Henry Atkins, 3A.

Henry was always in the top five. 'High-Five Henry' they would call him, and he excelled in the sciences and anything to do with computers or electronics in general. He even looked like a computer geek. Tall and thin, his angular arms producing bony elbows used as weapons of mass destruction as and when required in any given queue.

His particular favourite queue was the school tuck shop, frequented by Henry and his friends at break time every day. The 1p Jammy dodger the number one favourite of all the lads. Henry's face belied his tender years; shaving daily now, but he liked to leave a remnant of stubble which complemented his piercing grey eyes. He had a permanent studious look about him which suggested a certain knowledge, a twitch of his face and a stare that said 'of course I know how to do that'. In fact, Henry usually did know how to do a lot of things. His particular interest being electronics, he was extremely interested to hear about Banfield Grammar's new scheme, to install CCTV cameras in all classrooms. The grammar school not exactly a hotbed of hooliganism, but the newly elected Coalition government were quite hard-line about security, and they had invested heavily, via the Education Secretary, in school security. When a teacher has to leave the classroom for any reason, he or she presses a button and the security guy in Mission Control doesn't actually take over, but at least he can spot any untoward shenanigans, so to speak.

Henry spent the next few months investigating the development of the new systems. He had an older friend who worked for Edu-Secure, the consultants installing the systems. By the time the autumn term started, he had not only accessed the firm's internal database, but he'd already downloaded the schematics and operator's manual. Plus, the passwords to access the system.

'How you gonna do it, High-Five?'

'Easy. Log into the system, pick up a video recording of Mr Jones teaching us last week. Then I'll change the date and time and when we're ready I'll set the systems to activate the recordings so the security guy will actually be looking at last week's lesson.'

'What's the point of that?'

'Dumbo. That means we can do what the hell we like in the class while that recording is on the CCTV screen.'

'Nice one. What then?' said William Green.

'We'll kidnap Mr Jones.'

'What?'

'You heard. Four or five of us could overpower him easy. I've got nothing against him personally, but it's something we've talked about before.'

'Where would we take him, and how do we get him out of school?'

'For starters, I'll program the cameras with a 5-minute delay, then we'll bundle him down the corridor. Just got to avoid the Head and the Deputy. You know what they're like.'

The conversation continued for over 20 minutes, with others joining in to add to the plan. The main players in 3A had once been challenged by some younger students to do something outrageous, like 'hold a teacher to ransom'. Ok, we'll do it, they said. Henry would be in charge of the technical stuff. Mick, Bob and Simon would be the muscle. They'd handle old Jones easily. Gag him; tie him up, down a short corridor (not usually alarmed) and into a van driven by Mick's older brother, Sam.

The day arrived. Tuesday morning, double Maths with Mr Jones. The Deputy's on a course and the Head is in a long meeting. Henry accessed the Outlook diary in about 2 minutes flat once he'd found the School Secretary's password (sorry, Office Manager – Henry was always being picked up on political correctness). Ideal time to do this, everyone agreed.

10.00 a.m. The time had come. Mick gave the signal, and Henry ran the App on his phone. Within a minute he triggered the re-program of the security system, pre-set the night before. Arnold, the semi-retired security officer, sat there with his crossword and an endless supply of Mars and Snicker bars (he claimed to prefer Marathon), oblivious to the super-crime about to descend upon Banfield Grammar, established 1898. The school, that is, not the crime.

Henry coughed twice, the final signal. Mick, Bob and Simon pounced on the unsuspecting Mr Jones. Before he could shout for help, Mick stuffed a handkerchief in his mouth and wrapped thick black tape round his face, while others sat on him and bound his arms behind his back. Two of the younger students made sure the coast was clear.

'Ok Mick, go go go,' said William.

'For God's sake Will, it's not the A-Team.'

'Is the van there?'

'Yes, Sam's got the back door open and the engine's running.'

They bundled Mr Jones into the corridor and pushed him, shuffling and struggling towards the caretaker's room, and out of the side-door before anyone could see them. The van was parked round the corner by the bins. Henry continued to watch the CCTV images on his smart phone.

'Everything ok, High-Five?'

'No probs.'

'Let's go.'

They drove across the estate to a lock-up rented by Sam. As soon as they got him settled, Mick made the call.

'Put the Head Master on the phone now.'

The Head, Roger Simner, came to the phone, watched over by a very flustered Office Manager, Miss Hopkins.

'This is Roger Simner, what's all this about?'

'Mr Simner. We have Mr Jones, your Maths teacher. If you don't deliver £10,000 in twenty pound notes by 5.00 p.m. tomorrow, you won't see him again. Do not call the police.'

'Christ Mick', said Henry, 'that's not what we agreed. It's supposed to be a giggle.'

'Sod it. I've had enough of this damn school,' Mick said, holding his hand over the phone.

'Who is this?'

'Never mind who this is; can you get the money?'

Simner put the phone down. He knew who they were. How can they be so stupid? He called the police who took no more than an hour to track the call and surround the lock-up. They didn't understand why it was so easy. The 'gang' had made no attempt to disguise the phone number or their whereabouts. Within two hours Mr Jones was free and the four lads were in the interview room at Banfield station.

'What the hell were you playing at?' said Detective Sergeant Haskins.

'We're not playing,' said Henry; 'there's a point to this.'

'Explain.'

'What no one seems to realise is that the funding transferred to the school three months ago was not only sanctioned by Roger Simner's brother at the Local Education office, but also his brother-in-law runs Edu-Secure. Nice work if you can get it,' said Henry.

'So it's not just a scam, bit of a laugh, as your friend Mick claimed?'

'Might be to them, but I've been tracking Simner for some time. He's corrupt, and it goes to the top of the education department, and I can prove it.'

Prove it he did. Simner's career was abruptly ended, and a jail sentence followed, together with his brother and brother-in-law. Mick, Bob, Simon and Sam had no idea what Henry Atkins was up to. They wouldn't have understood anyway. Henry approached both his parents and the police months before when he had discovered the kind of man Simner was. Unfortunately, he'd done this by tapping Simner's phone. Not only was that illegal (they let it go as Henry was barely fourteen) but also it all sounded too incredible. Now, Henry had forced the issue. Poor old Mr Jones (an easy, but innocent, target) had been used in this elaborate scheme, but now the police would have to listen, and take action, which they did. Henry had bribed some second-year students to approach the 3A gang and challenge them to carry out the kidnap. It suited his purposes, and he was not afraid to use anyone, even his closest friends, to bring corrupt officials to justice.

Henry was destined for higher things. He quite fancied the idea of joining MI5, but there's just one little matter to get out of the way first. GCSE exams.

The Journey

'Think we've got a flat tyre,' the woman said.

'You're right.'

Sam had been driving for over half an hour and didn't even know her name. This was the first meaningful thing she'd said. All he had heard so far was 'I'm having tints in my hair tomorrow' (whatever tints are, he thought) and that she must, 'really must', give up smoking. She wasn't smoking now, and she seemed nice enough.

'I'll pull over and have a look.'

Luckily, he hadn't got one of those new-fangled cars with no spare. You know the sort of thing, when the salesman tells you what a great idea it is to have a flat tyre and pump a couple of litres of white sticky stuff into the tyre only to find that it deflates as soon as you set off. Thank God for the AA, he thought.

'You ok; need any help?'

'No thanks, won't be long, just putting the spare on.'

I should have asked her to get out of the car, he thought, but it's drizzling and cold. I'll take the chance it might come off the jack.

'All done, sorry about that.'

'Forgot to say, do you know where you're going,' she said.

'What do you mean; I thought you said you lived out this way.'

'I know, I just wanted to get away, and you seemed nice.'

'Not sure I understand. Where do you want to go?'

'Anywhere. Just away from that place.'

He knew what she meant. He had been going there for six months himself and had lost track of why he bothered to turn up every Thursday morning. Most of what he heard was a load of rubbish, but it did seem to dull the pain. One year tomorrow she had died. I don't just miss her, he thought, I ache for her.

'You remind me of my husband. We were parted some time ago. I thought the group would help.'

'Know what you mean.'

Silence took over for a full hour. They drove on. He didn't care anymore. They saw the sign for the next service station twenty minutes after they joined the M5 southbound. He didn't know what they were doing, where they were going.

In the group, they had hardly exchanged any words, just a mumbled 'good morning' like everyone else. Now they were together, and it didn't seem unnatural. They stopped in the cafe for egg and chips which he covered with his favourite brown sauce after doing battle with the 'easy to open' plastic container - the sort of thing you really need scissors for, like a sachet of shampoo. She smiled at his vain efforts to tear off the corner and eventually touched his hand as if to say 'I'll do it for you.'

Back on the motorway, his thoughts drifted towards the future. What happens next. He should be concerned that he really has no idea who this woman is, and she doesn't appear to know him. He looked across at her, imagining that she seemed to have changed. Her face was softer, kinder. No longer a stranger. She smiled. At that moment he felt he knew her and they still hadn't exchanged names, talked about where they lived, what they did for a living.

'Get off at this junction.'

He didn't argue. They were now on a country lane, God knows where, and he could see the light fading.

'We'll have to stop at some point.'

'Keep going for now, I'm happy just to be here.'

'Do you know where we are?'

'We'll be approaching a small village called Deebury in the next twenty minutes or so.'

'How do you know?' he said.

No answer, but she smiled, and he accepted that. Lights on, sun falling in the sky, he was getting tired.

'Hang on, Deebury you say?   I've been there before.'

A memory from many years before sparked through his brain. They had stayed in a small village for two nights on the way to Newquay before they were married.

'How did you...'

'Sam, it's me,' she said.

66

The Birthday Present

'Please Dad, you promised.'

'We'll see. It's a lot of money.'

'Only £420.'

'Only. That should be enough for four birthdays and a few Christmas presents thrown in for good measure.'

Greg really did want the new B-Box Superama Game Panel, alternatively known as the FX600. According to Greg, the extra bonus was that it's Windows 10 compatible. Greg's Dad, Jeff, said the technology passed him by. He reluctantly played the occasional computer game with his son, and had made an extra effort over the last year since Greg's Mom finally succumbed to the cancer that had taken over their lives. He wanted to do as much as possible for his son, and he could just about afford it. His only doubt was that he might be spoiling him, replacing the endless time and love that Katie had given them both.

Jeff had worked for Griffin Plating for twenty years, progressing from junior fitter to senior engineer. Responsible for the production of anything that fits on the outside of a car - bumpers, door embellishers, handles; he was well paid. Fortunately, after Katie died, his boss offered him a promotion so the extra money compensated for the loss of Katie's part-time earnings at the local library.

He enjoyed his job, and lucky that his son was just old enough to find his way from school on his own. Twelve in eight weeks' time, Greg preferred to walk home with his mates anyway. His Mom used to collect him, but he learned to look after himself for part of the day. Jeff felt a little guilty, but there was no one else available to help, and he couldn't take time off during the day for the school runs. The factory demanded working hours of 8.30 a.m. to 5.00 p.m., with an hour for lunch. Somehow, they coped and enjoyed a good father / son relationship. On the odd occasion, Greg would play up if he felt that his mates were doing better than him. Most of them owned an FX600. Simon, his best mate, had an FX600 Deluxe class 2, but both his parents were dentists. Jeff couldn't compete with that, and Greg was mature enough to understand. On the question of the 'basic' FX600, there was no argument. Jeff had promised him one for his birthday, not realising at the time the price tag exceeded £400. He still had the mortgage to pay and in arrears to the tune of £1500 on his credit card. The interest payments mounted up, but he would be able to take on some more overtime to cover that.

'Come in Jeff, sit down,' Mr Atkins pointed to a spare seat in his office.

'Everything ok Mr Atkins? Nothing wrong on the motor production line I hope.'

'No, it's not that Jeff. We're very pleased with the quality of your work. Problem is, Holmer Cars announced last night at their AGM that they're selling out to the Chinese. All the production is moving to Peking and they have local suppliers for the fittings. All their production workers are being laid off. They're only retaining a sales office for the UK.'

'How does that affect us?'

'We would lose over 30% of our total sales. I'm afraid the motor production line has to close. Holmer is our largest client, over 80% of motor sales. It's not cost-effective to carry on the line.'

'What's the bottom-line Mr Atkins?'

'Sorry Jeff, we'll have to make you redundant. I'll see the other lads later today. There is something else. Head Office have told me that your break in service will affect your redundancy entitlement.'

'But I couldn't help my wife being ill.'

'I know, I'm so sorry, my hands are tied. On a technicality you left our employment. We kept the job open for you, but it means you only have one year's service. You don't qualify for redundancy.'

'That can't be right. You're writing off eighteen years, and I was only away for ten months.'

'Listen Jeff, personally I agree with you. I've made a case and they won't listen. You're not in a union, but you have the option of instructing a solicitor.'

'Stuff that, I can't get legal aid. You know I can't. For Christ sake, is there nothing you can do?'

Jeff spent the next few weeks investigating where he stood. Even Acas said his case was legally weak, although morally the firm owed him more. He had no choice but to accept it. He left within the month, four weeks before Greg's birthday, and signed on for Job Seekers Allowance.

'Greg, mate, I'm so sorry, the FX600 is going to have to wait.'

'You can't Dad, you promised.'

'Please understand son, we can't afford it.'

'If Mom was here, she'd sort it.'

Jeff was upset for his son, who had set his heart on the new games machine, but the mortgage and credit card payments must come first. Get sorted, get another job, and maybe for Christmas...

Greg used to go to church every week with his Mom, and on occasions they would go in during the week for morning prayers, a cup of coffee always waiting for them in the church hall. Aware that Greg had continued the routine, he rarely attended himself. As it was half-term, Greg was free to go along on both Tuesday and Thursday prayer mornings, starting at 10.00 a.m. Unable to go after he lost Katie, Jeff somehow blamed the church for not doing more. He also blamed himself, but it was the dreadful disease, not individuals, that had taken her. On Tuesday morning, Greg went on his own, then for some reason Jeff decided to tag along on Thursday. He didn't tell Greg, and set out five minutes after Greg left the house.

Greg sat in his usual place, third pew from the front on the right hand side. He was kneeling with his head down when Jeff walked into the back of the church. He sat four rows behind Greg, but he could hear everything he said.

'Please God, I wish you'd been able to save my Mom. She didn't deserve to suffer, and what have we done to deserve this? I don't ask for much, and I don't blame Dad, but he's lost his job. Is there any way you can do something for us? It's not just the FX600, but it would be nice. To be honest, if you could help Dad with his debts, I'd be prepared to wait for the new machine.'

Jeff's eyes filled with tears. Far from being angry, he was so proud of his son, just eleven years of age, and displayed such maturity. He lowered himself into the pew and knelt down, not initially intending to pray, but mainly to avoid the embarrassment of Greg seeing him there. What Jeff didn't see was someone sitting just two rows behind him, listening to everything Greg said, and then followed with interest a similar plea from Jeff.

'Why did you have to take her? You should have taken me instead. I'm not bothered about money or anything for myself, but look how it's affecting Greg.'

Jeff waited for Greg to leave the church, sat for a few minutes, then made his way home. The next day he resumed job searching, and the same routine continued for the next three weeks. Nothing. No jobs available, and his credit card bill now approached £2500. They'd cut back on everything. Their meals were more basic than before. The night before his birthday, Greg sat on the settee with Jeff.

'Don't worry Dad, I don't expect anything. I understand how it is. We've both been let down, but it's not your fault.'

The next morning, Greg opened his present. The latest Olly Murs CD and the new Doctor Who Annual.

'Thanks Dad, they're great.'

Jeff had to turn away, he felt so ashamed.

The door bell rang.

'Eight in the morning; who on earth's that?'

Jeff opened the front door leading to the porch. In his more affluent period he would often have books and DVDs delivered via on-line purchases specifying delivery instructions of 'please leave in porch, do not leave next door'. It was a large parcel, addressed to Greg Ashburn, 26 Field Avenue, Banfield. A small blue envelope had been attached. Strange, he thought, if that's a birthday card you'd think it would be *inside* the parcel. Delivery drivers don't usually attach birthday cards. He carried the parcel into the kitchen.

'What is it Dad?'

'It's for you.'

Unable to contain his excitement, he ripped open the parcel. Jeff held onto the envelope, noticing a smell. Not unpleasant, on the contrary. He put it to his nose. No, it couldn't be; that perfume. He placed it next to the parcel.

'Crikey Dad, you won't believe this. It's the B-Box FX600!'

Greg opened the envelope, finding a plain white card. On it were printed two words.

'Honeybunch. Enjoy.'

Greg realised straight away, and hugged his Dad, crying openly.

'Dad, that's what Mom used to call me.'

'I know son, I don't understand...'

Greg went off to school, leaving Jeff in a daze. He sat in the kitchen, staring at the note, wishing he could go back two years and change things; maybe go to church more, anything. Was this a sign? The phone rang. Mr Atkins came straight to the point.

'Head Office contacted me this morning, Jeff. They've had a change of heart. There's still no job, but you will, after all, be entitled to twenty weeks' redundancy pay. That's nearly £8000 tax free. I'll send a confirmation letter in the post today.'

'But why, what's changed?'

'It's very sad, but the Managing Director's wife received some test results yesterday. She's been diagnosed with terminal cancer. He told me that he now understands what you went through, and this is the least he can do. He still feels guilty about the way you were treated, and he hopes you will forgive him.'

'Tell him there's nothing to forgive, and please tell him that if he wants someone to talk to, I would be prepared to help him get through it. It's the least I can do...'

Victor

My wife calls me Victor Meldrew. You can probably guess why, but I'll explain anyway. Yes, middle-aged grumpy old man, but the things that happen to me are not my fault. People in modern life simply do stuff, and it drives me mad. Mind you, I didn't expect it all to happen in one day...

The day started well enough - managed to get through to 8.30 a.m. without setting fire to Julie's new kitchen. I call her Julie, as that's her official name, but secretly I think of her as Margaret. Well, if she can call me Victor, I'll reply in kind with 'Margaret Meldrew'. From what I remember of the sitcom, she was actually the more bad-tempered of the two; things just happened to poor old Victor. I'm the same. Anyway, as I say, the kitchen survived two rounds of toast and a boiled egg, I didn't fall down the stairs, and Margaret (sorry, Julie) didn't leave drawing pins on the kitchen chair. In reality she's never done that, but there's always a first time.

Now, it would be nice, for once, just for once, if I could step out of my front door and not be confronted with what seems like the back-end of a rubbish cart or the local tip. It only seems to happen to us. Trevor next door thinks because we're the last house in the row (just before a clump of conifers) the wind blows that way and we cop for all the rubbish people have dropped. Reading that sentence back I don't think I meant to say 'rubbish people'. On reflection however...

As my Dad used to say 'any road up for a pound of feathers', I stepped out of the porch and counted at least six different items of rubbish. Empty film cartridge packet, empty coke tin, yoghurt pot (one, empty), fish and chip wrapping (funny that, not newspaper), what I thought was a condom, but no, it was a balloon, and the usual Embassy no. 10 (empty). No one ever leaves a FULL can of coke, 20 ciggies, hot fish or a chip, a new tub of vanilla Muller Lite and an unused film for a Kodak Ektra camera. I looked up and down the road. Trevor next door – immaculate drive and front lawn; Chris and Kate next door to Trevor – same; Pete and Samantha three doors down - not one bit of rubbish. Charming. I don't mind sharing.

That bloody tree outside next door's house has been dropping its flaming leaves all year. Not just in the autumn, but particularly through the summer. Phoned the Council – no interest.

'But the tree's virtually dead.'

'Sorry sir, can't go and look at every tree someone complains about; not unless it's considered to be a hazard.'

'No, but I will be at this rate.'

82

'Sorry sir?'

'Never mind, forget it.'

I wouldn't mind, but our drive and particularly my car seems to attract the sticky sap that oozes from the stalks and leaves that fall from the damn thing. Washed my car three times last week. Notice that they seem to avoid Trevor's car.

Don't get me started on slugs and snails. All over the lawn today. Seventeen mixed varieties I counted. They're for it. Don't care if the RSPCA come round, or shouldn't that be the RSPCS. Bloody things. Ruined my petunias. I've tried pellets, salt, even beer in a saucer (my dear old Mom's idea). They just drink the beer and stagger off. Must think it's a snail pub crawl. I'll have a word with Mom about that at the weekend. Where does she get these ideas; Mrs Beaton or something? Yes, and while we're on the subject of gardens; why is it that every pigeon within a five-mile radius decided to get together and dive bomb my brand new fences just after I'd painted them? I've never seen so much pigeon crap. Again, big surprise, only **my** fences.

Now there's another surprise. Talking about the pigeons, every dog owner on the estate has brought their dogs to, once again, visit the pavement outside our house. What the hell are they giving them to eat? Last week I used a full bottle of Dettol cleaning the pavement. Mrs Jones in the next street complained about the smell. She obviously prefers Eau-de-Dog-poo.

Crikey, I've only been out of the house five minutes, not even reached my car, and there's a catalogue of the usual stuff. It's not that I have a persecution complex, but I'm sure they're out to get me. Even Bill Greats (is he still at Bimosoft?) had a go at me just before I came out. Well, sort of.

Those bloody software updates he sends that bugger up my nice tidy computer system. Things that were working before don't work now. Thanks Bill. Julie says you've retired, but it was you that formed the company. I still blame you. I'll have to do yet another system restore when I get back from my optician's appointment. I just know it will be another arm and a leg (probably two legs). By the way, going back to the dog owners, I've just noticed some dog mess on my lawn! It's that daft old chap with the extendable dog lead. If I catch him letting that scruffy Scottie on my property once more...

In the car, trying to stay calm. No good your blood pressure going through the roof. Might confuse the girl who tests your eye pressure before you go in to see Mr Biggins.
Watch out, there's one! Another flaming school kid on a bike mounting the pavement. Good grief, nearly hit that old lady. Shouldn't be allowed.

Happened last week as I was reversing out of the drive. I'm trying my best not to run into them, but why can't they stay on the road or mount the pavement somewhere else? Now, here we go again. I'm at the lights and there's this big stupid lorry driver who can't help himself; inching forward bit by bit trying to get as close to my rear bumper as possible. He must know I only bought the car last week. Must be the reason. Jealousy. Why else would he almost get the front of his lorry into my boot? Stuck my fingers up to him last time. Shut my electric window just in time and the lights changed to green as he got out of his cab. Prat. Tail-gating should be banned. Heavy fines.

Two hundred and fifty quid. I'd be better off with a magnifying glass, but Mr Biggins says the DVLC wouldn't allow that while I'm driving. Funny. Two hundred and fifty quid though. No wonder he's driving around in that big silver Audi. Nice car, but I'm paying for that. I'll collect the new specs next week. At least I'll be able to read the small print on my latest mobile phone contract. Have you seen what they put in those documents? And another thing, last time I phoned they kept me on hold for over twenty minutes listening to Greensleeves, or the Planet Suite or something like that. All sounds the same to me. Back home now. What's this, bank statement. What? That can't be right; I'll phone them straight away. God, Greensleeves. They must have the same system as the mobile phone people... Fifteen minutes now, could be going for the record.

'You are in a queue. Sorry that our operatives are all busy. Your call is important to us; thank you so much for waiting. By the way, all calls will be recorded for training purposes when you eventually get through.'

Oh stuff it, I won't bother. Too busy. Anyway, Julie's left me a note.

'Hi Love, please phone the washing machine people. Packed up again just after you went out. I've left the contact details on your desk. See you later. Empty tub. Don't want a flood.'

No, I couldn't stand another call centre. Not just yet. She'll be back just after lunch. Maybe she'll... get a grip, have faith. I'll just leave it for a bit.

Door bell's ringing. Who's that now?

'Good morning sir. I've noticed that your roof tiles, and the plastic facia around your windows need some attention.'

'Have you now.'

'Have you considered investing in new facia and having the tiles replaced?'

'Sod off.'

That sorted him. He's been three times in the last month. What's this on the floor. More junk mail. BerklyCard. I don't even bank with them. For pity's sake, I don't want a credit card. I've already got one. Right. This lot's going straight back to them marked 'not known at this address'. I should do that every time. No, I might as well phone about the washing machine. 0207, 643... It's ringing. Oh God, Greensleeves... Can't do this, I'm mow the front lawn and sort it when she's back.

'Hi love, I'm back. What are you doing out the front? Engineer come yet?'

'No, I couldn't get through. You know what they're like.'

'How long ago was that? How long have you been out the front?'

'Why?'

'You did empty the machine like I asked you, didn't you?'

'In your note, you said empty tub, don't want a flood. Thought you meant you'd emptied the tub.'

'Oh my God, let's get inside quick.'

'Crikey, sorry Julie, bit of a mess isn't it?'

'Victor !!!'

Big Fish in a Small Pool

David White, midfield, Wolverhampton Wanderers. Sounds good, if it could be that way. Sometimes an apparent talent or just being a dominant character in a primary school proves the old saying 'big fish in a small pool'. David was no exception.

David's infant and primary school career became a fast-track process; reading fluently when he started Ploughman's Green Primary just before his fifth birthday. Few kids reached that level in their first year. David was already taking in the front page news of the daily paper and rattling through 'Janet and John' like the books had gone out of fashion. It helped having an older sister. Liz a great help to him as she also went to Ploughman's Green and was in year four when he joined the reception class. By the time David reached the age of seven, Liz was teaching him French. At that point, she was a prefect in the final primary year and had quite a skill for languages and also teaching. David enjoyed his time at Ploughman's Green. He coped with every intellectual obstacle put in his way and excelled at the basics - mental arithmetic, reading, writing and grammar. However, from the age of eight, football dominated his life. His Dad, Norman (and his father before him) as a fanatical Wolves fan, this very easily rubbed off on his son, but playing remained David's priority. Not particularly highly skilled in terms of ball control, he nonetheless dominated every match both in the playground and on the field in competitive school games. He could play anywhere, but most comfortable in midfield. He would say 'just behind the strikers'.

When not playing football at school, he would use every waking hour at home trying to perfect various skills. Kicking a tennis ball against the side of the house (while annoying his Mom, Sally) gave him the opportunity to alternate his 'kicking foot', trying not to be too 'right-sided'. His left foot quite weak – he could trap the ball ok, but a smooth drive through with the left instep did not compete with his right foot. This is where his beloved sister, Liz, wasn't much help. English and French, fine, but football - she hated it, so David ploughed a lonely furrow most spring and summer evenings in the back garden.

Academically, David started to excel, and after year two he progressed straight through to year four, together with Winston and Jennifer, also considered to be advanced beyond their years. This meant that, as he progressed from infants to the junior school, he attended a class of children physically larger than him, but intellectually on a par. From the point of view of sport, he was quite small and thin, but he had tremendous speed, agility, with boundless energy and stamina.

School and football were not the only important aspects for David in the 1960s. Holidays added the bonus of fun to his life. His Mom, Dad, sister and the dog, Rex, helped to make every holiday an adventure. For what seemed like every year for ever, they went camping in Borth, on the west coast of Wales. Camping disasters ever present, but one year was particularly terrible, resulting in Norman, shall we say, less than pleased.

'They've supplied the wrong bloody poles, brand new sodding tent.'

'Norman, please don't swear.'

'What the flamin' eck do you expect, Sally?'

'The children, please.'

'I don't mind, Mom,' David piped up.

'Shut up now David,' Norman was not in the mood.

So, for two consecutive years, the family found themselves unable to use a tent. They ended up in a scruffy little caravan (Norman didn't quite describe it that way). Taken over by spiders that had done a wonderful job weaving their webs across and down the internal contours of the caravan; 'the box of death' Norman called it. David regarded it as another great adventure. The previous year they had to abandon ship (an apt phrase in the circumstances) when the rains came and stubbornly refused to go away. The White clan, together with eight other intrepid camping families, spent four glorious days and nights together in the local community centre. Before the swift exit from the bottom of the flooded field (seven inches deep although Sally alleged three feet), David fascinated to find Rex, quite well and happy, sitting on the spare lilo bobbing around in the water. Fortunately for the Whites, at that stage the inner tent they slept in was uphill enough to avoid four wet bottoms first thing in the morning.

Down to the beach most mornings for Norman, David and Liz; the only time that Liz would engage in the 'stupid' (her words) sports of football and cricket. David, in his element, took great pleasure in hitting six after six, making Liz work very hard retrieving the ball. The rule in beach cricket - 'in the sea it's six'. David made sure, when Liz was fielding, the stumps were placed just close enough to blast one into the water. She can swim, what's the problem, he thought.

On another holiday, this time in Aberystwyth (10 miles from Borth), the White family had quite an interesting time. You could say that the dog tried to commit suicide and they met the future King of England. Saying it like that suggests a link, and there is no link, but an element of truth runs through both stories, except no actual evidence that Rex (the dog, that is, whose name happens to be Latin for 'King') actually intended to hurt himself. Mind you, we'll never know.

The dog first. Mom, Dad and the two kids visiting Aberystwyth Castle, built during the first Welsh War in the late 13th Century. Norman and Sally sat down on a bench near one of the D-shaped towers and Sally opened the flask she always carried, so a cup of tea is never far away. David, Liz and Rex went off to explore the tower, part of the inner ward's gatehouse keep. They ran from room to room, Rex following every step. In the castle keep, on the second level about twenty feet above the path, there was an opening, an old window which appeared to have a stone bench built into the wall. David and Liz had run into the adjoining room and Rex launched himself onto the bench and bounced straight through the window opening, thinking he was chasing the kids. Unfortunately, it was a sheer drop.

It took them a few minutes to realise what had happened. Both of the children burst into tears when they saw the dog, motionless, on the ground. They rushed downstairs and screamed out to Norman.

'Dad, help, please help!'

'What the hell happened?'

'He was chasing after us - he jumped straight through that window. Is he going to be ok?'

Norman judged that a ticking off would not be the appropriate reaction to this situation, and he ran over to see if Rex had survived the fall, but expecting serious injuries at the very least. Unconscious for a few minutes, he then came round, blood oozing from his mouth. Norman carefully picked him up and carried him over the road to the beach. The children followed, and watched their father gently place the dog down and then splash sea-water over his mouth. They sat on the beach for over twenty minutes, and gradually Rex seemed to recover. He was limping and had a nasty swelling in his mouth and his gums still bleeding. Some teeth missing. Norman found a local vet who checked if Rex had sustained any serious injury.

'Two teeth gone, but he's been very lucky. I'll give you a tube of ointment to rub into his gums to prevent infection. He's probably bruised the bone in his leg, but nothing broken.'

The miracle of the leaping dog out of the way, Norman and Sally had a surprise for the children. Last year (1967), Prince Charles had been admitted to study at Trinity College Cambridge but he planned to spend one term in his second year at the University College of Wales in Aberystwyth to study Welsh history and language. His mother had made him Prince of Wales in 1958 and his investiture at Caernarfon Castle not due until 1969, so this presented him with the opportunity to learn the basics of the language. The exciting thing for the White family was that tomorrow Charles would attend his first day at college. Security may not have been as tight in those days, and they managed to find out what time he planned to arrive - 10.30 a.m. David didn't appreciate the significance of the occasion and would have been more interested if George Best had been joining the college. He'd make do with Prince Charles.

10.15 a.m., the whole White family are lined up on the steps of the college. Sally and Liz could not contain their excitement. Just before 10.30 a.m. an open-top E-Type pulled up, the twenty-year-old prince driving, with his detective as the passenger. Charles handed the keys to a college official as he got out of the car and walked up the steps. Sally pushed David forward.

'Touch him; he's the future King of England.'

'No way Mom, you touch him.'

Charles simply smiled and ruffled David's hair. Liz did an impromptu curtsy (a sneer from David to Liz that said 'pillock') and Norman nodded as Sally beamed with pride. Within seconds he breezed through the main doors, followed by the detective, and the future King of England disappeared from their lives.

'Don't you realise who that was?' said Sally.

'Crikey Mom, you've been going on about it since breakfast. Big deal.'

'History. That's what it is. History in the making,' said Norman.

Back in school, David became very competitive with his fellow pupils, especially with Jennifer and Winston. The trio, all aged eight, effectively the alpha stream of bright children who had skipped a year and were now in the same class as nine-year-olds. The competition particularly fierce with Winston. After all, thought David, Jenny's a girl, and she's really nice, but Winston's a pain. David was no racist, but unfortunately Winston always wanted to point out the colour difference. It usually meant nothing to David, but one day he snapped. Winston once more droned on about 'whites thinking they are better' and David went for him. The kids in the playground gathered round and Jenny tried to intervene.

'Leave him David; he's just winding you up.'

David grabbed Winston's throat, two shirt buttons flying off in the process.

'If you say anything about whites again I'll smash your face in.'

'Leave me alone!'

Winston hit out and caught David on his left cheek. David turned, kicked Winston hard, connecting firmly with his right knee. Winston started to cry, and as David pushed him over, Mr Simons rushed over and dragged him away.

'What on earth are you doing?'

'He started it.'

'Both of you to Mr Smith's study. Now!'

After a stern lecture, a hand-shake, and two young boys promising there would be no repeat of the incident, Winston and David initially, reluctantly, sealed the truce. In fact, for the rest of their time at Ploughman's Green they became firm friends. Both had learned something about equality and respect. Both of them intelligent lads, they realised there was nothing wrong with healthy competition, and didn't need to come to blows.

By the age of nine, David's football career began to take off, selected as a substitute for the match against Anderton Green, on the outskirts of Banfield. Younger and certainly thinner (but not shorter) than all the players on either side, he made his entrance in the second half. His superior pace and movement obvious, even though ball control was not his greatest attribute. On a number of occasions, he took the ball past two or three players, shooting at will and scored two goals.

After a three-one win and a great improvement in the vibrancy of the team's performance in the second half, David was selected as right-sided midfield for the next match. He kept his place in the team for the rest of the season.

The following year David reached the 'top class', the final year when the Eleven Plus would be taken, but football continued to be his top priority. By Christmas he was appointed as the youngest ever team captain of Ploughman's Green, already top scorer with nine goals. Then, his dream of playing for beloved Wolves came even closer.

The sports teacher Mr Lester was contacted by the chief coach of Wolverhampton Wanderers, Sammy Chung. Bill McGarry, the first team manager, had given Chung the task of sourcing new local talent, the theory being that if the club could find eleven-year-olds with potential and get the parents to sign what was then called 'schoolboy forms', they could retain the small minority that might make it through to professional ranks. Every primary school in the borough had been contacted but the news given to David by Mr Lester about the up-coming trial made him feel very special. Another life lesson was looming. The day came, and the best three players in the team - David, the goal-keeper Adrian Westwood and the left-winger Keith Banks trooped out onto the field in their green jerseys and white shorts. Awaiting them Sammy Chung, his two assistants and Mr Lester. David convinced himself that his opportunity had arrived, and his dream of becoming a professional footballer almost a reality. David was thrilled when Sammy Chung took him to one side.

'I'll work with you David. Adrian, Keith, go over to the other side of the penalty area. My assistants will work with you.'

The next five minutes were the most exciting of David's short life. It was simple. Sammy Chung threw the ball towards him, and, as instructed, he chested it down, and side-footed it towards the coach. Again, left foot this time. No problem. Repeat, right foot, then left.

'Thanks David, that's all.'

He was convinced that he had passed the trial, and the following morning Mr Lester called him to his office to discuss how he had faired.

'You did really well David. Mr Chung was impressed. But there are so many good young footballers, they can't take them all.'

'What about the others?'

'Well, Keith has been asked to go to Molineux for a second trial.'

The world seemed to fall away from David at that moment. His dream shattered, he simply could not understand, after being top-scorer, the youngest ever captain. He knew he was good. It turned out that any decent professional coach can tell as soon as you touch the football. Chesting it down and knocking it back seemed easy. They can tell from your style and posture whether you have the makings of a professional. David was good, at that level, but his football career would not progress beyond appearing for school teams.

'Devastated' might be over-playing how he felt about it, but as he had planned his whole life around playing football, it came pretty close. Lessons learned, and this helped to shape the man he became. He was not to find life easy in the future, but his experiences made him stronger. As he moved towards adolescence, he gradually became more comfortable as a small fish in an ever increasing pool.

The Man in The Shed

He was there again this morning. That's five days now; not sure how we'll get rid of him. Personally, I don't mind someone kipping in our garden, but Barbara annoys me with her hypocritical views. First, she doesn't want him there, then she complains if I suggest drastic measures. If it was up to me, I'd leave him there, as long as he doesn't tread on my petunias.

'You'll have to do something Ted.'

'Exactly what do you expect me to do.'

'Don't know, but you're the man of the house.'

Fine. I went through the options.

1)   Call the police – they won't be interested unless he ravishes Barbara or steals the family silver (which doesn't exist).She perked up when I mentioned the bit about the ravishing.

2)   Tackle him ourselves - this could involve negotiation, physical violence, bribery, corruption, blackmail, mediation or a combination of all these things. Mediation

seems a bit cruel, anyhow. The poor bugger might have to endure a social worker type and that just wouldn't do.

3)   Ask around to see if anyone knows him and negotiate a transfer fee – not a good option either.   Our neighbours aren't interested in anything, apart from Corrie and Emmerdale. Try phoning them between 7.00 p.m. and 8.00 p.m. most nights.

4)   Leave him be.

What would you do?

'We'll play the long game,' I said.

'What on earth do you mean?'

'Leave him for a bit, then get to know him and see if there's a gentle way of persuading him to give us our shed back.'

'Well...' the helpful comment from my good lady wife.

The long game it is. Three days went by, and we think he's looking a bit thin and peaky. Barbara took him sandwiches and a flask of tea.

'No sugar next time please,' he said, 'I can't stand sugar.'

Two weeks go by and far from being irritated by the scruffy stranger in the shed, we've become quite fond of him. Don't think Barbara would be bothered if I went and he stayed.

'Why don't we ask him in for a meal? He could have a bath first. He seems so lonely and I'm sure he'll be no trouble.'

My first reaction was to pick up the Telegraph, light my pipe and make a grumbling, snorting sound. Barbara says she doesn't like the way my jowls wobble when I'm in a huff. I didn't bother to make the old joke; the retort that's it's a Fiat 500 we're got and not a huff. Not the Mark 2, anyway. After calming down and realising what side my bread's buttered, I agreed that Mr Whatsisname (we must ask him) could have a bath and then join us for a meal.

A cosy arrangement developed for... yes, we know his name now.

'Mr Wallburger. Please call me Mr Wallburger. Don't like to be too familiar, first names, that sort of thing.'

'Is there anything else you'd like us to do?'

'There is one thing. Since I started using your toilet instead of the one at the public baths in Queens Road, I have to knock your back door to get in. Sometimes you've gone out, and it's very inconvenient, if you get my drift.'

'Oh I get your drift, er, Mr Wallburger. What do you suggest?'

'Well, it would make more sense if I had a key to the back door.'

'What?'

'Be fair Ted; I don't think that's unreasonable. It's only three or four times a day.'

I'm not sure that all this was in the agreement at our nuptials twenty-five years ago. The vicar said 'in sickness and in health' and not 'thou shalt take in all the waifs and strays who ambush your garden shed.' However, Barbara was unanimous, and we don't live in a democracy in our house. We had a spare set of keys cut for him. The next demand came the following week.

'The Smiths at number fifty-four had Sky-Plus. You've only got Freeview. How can I watch Sky Atlantic films and the Premier League footy? You can afford it, Ted.'

Again Barbara found a way to justify his demands.

'You like the football, Ted, and you're always saying we should watch more movies. It's only £12 a month.'

'Yes, but who's paying for it? Muggins.'

Nevertheless, by the end of the month he had a set of keys, twice-weekly baths, two meals a day, Sky-Plus and my old pair of slippers. Another thing, I had to buy a new pipe. Mr Wallburger purloined my best pipe and four 50 gram tubs of my favourite Ashford Virginia. I'm beginning to wonder if he'll be sleeping with Barbara next. He winks at her a lot and she gives him that smile. The sort of smile that says something to a bloke. Something that she hasn't said to me in twenty years. I'm beginning to give up hope.

I needn't have worried. He won't be sleeping with my wife, or with me for that matter. I think he began to get tired of us. We would have to be quiet when Countdown was on.

'I'll have to wind it back now to hear what Nick Hewer has said. Shush this time; he's funny isn't he?'

I couldn't give a monkey's whatsit how hilarious the Countdown host is. He could jump on the desk naked, singing the National Anthem for all I care. It's my bloody telly.

'Anything wrong Ted?' he asked.

A glare from Barbara aimed piercingly straight at me, threateningly.

'No nothing, Mr Wallburger. Absolutely nothing.'

I glare back. Telepathic signals skewing into her brain saying 'I'm going to kill him in a minute.'

This goes on for weeks, until the fateful day. Our regular soiree to Sainsburys took a bit longer today. She wanted to stock up ready for next Christmas, and get the Easter eggs for our herd of nieces and nephews. All bloody nine of 'em. We've got no kids, but we shell out for everybody else's sprogs. Pulling into the drive now; everything looks ok. He hasn't sold the house while we've been shopping.

'You get the front door open and I'll empty the boot. The twenty-four cans of Guinness you've bought for our friend are particularly heavy and...'

'For God's sake, Ted, stop moaning and help me with the front door.'

'What do you mean, help?'

'The key won't fit.'

She was right. We go round the back and try that door. Same problem. He was at the window; pipe in mouth, Telegraph in one hand, Sky-Plus remote in the other. He opened the window.

'You know, the shed's not too bad this time of year. Give it a go. I've moved the two sun loungers from the spare bedroom and some blankets and cushions. You should be ok. It's for the best. Things were getting fraught, and we don't want to fall out, do we?'

'I...'

The words failed to appear. I swallowed them as Barbara glared at me. Probably all my fault. Maybe he'll let us use the bathroom once in a while...

Reunion for Ralph

Joseph was sad to hear about his old friend Ralph, who had developed dementia. He hadn't seen him for a few months but they had been very close, particularly all those years ago at Banfield Grammar. When the news about Ralph sunk in (he couldn't remember how he'd found out) he telephoned a few friends to see if there was anything they could do to help him.

'Hi Jack, have you heard about Ralph?'

'Yes, bad business, Alzheimer's, isn't it?'

'Think so. You know, we must do something.'

'What about a reunion for our old school, mates? We could raise some money for Ralph.'

'Crackin' idea mate. I'll ring Simon and Matt. You ring the others if you don't mind; at least the ones who are still around. We forget, it's been 45 years since we left the Grammar'.

Over the next few weeks, everyone rallied round, and a date was arranged for a reunion. Twenty-fifth of June, 1.00 p.m. at the Swan in Leeford Village, just outside Banfield. They do a nice buffet lunch, or fish and chips if the lads prefer that.

Joseph reminisced about his five years at the Grammar school. He could tell you the names of all the lads in his class, right back to 1C with Mr Carr. Nineteen Seventy an exciting year for Joseph - first year at senior school, trials for the cricket First Eleven. He was a decent bowler (right-arm spinner) and besides enjoying a variety of sports, he was thrilled by the academic challenges of subjects like Latin or Mathematics. Isn't it strange, Joseph thought, we must all be the same at our age; I very often can't find my car keys but I can remember the names of the teachers (even one of the dinner ladies) and my fellow pupils, and precise details about some of the lessons.

One day in the second year, Mr Morris organised a book auction. Mark Hill had brought in a book called 'Skinhead', worth about 5p. Not the sort of book Mom and Dad would like Joseph to be reading, but along with all the other lads in the class, Joseph knew there were swear words (page 57) and this was forbidden territory for a 12-year-old in those days. This was not the enlightened social-media driven 21st Century.

'I'll bid 10p,' said Simon.

'15p,' said Ralph.

Joseph came in at 20p, then 35p after several other bids from equally excited school-mates.

'55p,' shouted John Smith

'65p,' said Joseph.

No one else dared go any higher. For Joseph, that was three week's pocket money. He would have some explaining to do, but it would be worth it. There was a lot to learn about the world for lads of his age.

All these memories, with fine details, continued to flood back for Joseph. What time is it? What was he doing this morning? He remembered he was supposed to ring Ralph and arrange to go and see him. Sixty-one was not a big age, and really young to develop dementia. Joseph felt so lucky to be fit and well. Poor old Ralph.

A few weeks before the day of the reunion, Jack phoned Joseph and said that he had arranged everything. No need to worry, he'd spoken to the school and they had made a £50 donation towards the cost.

'You've been out of work the last two years, mate,' he said to Joseph.

'No need to pay anything.'

'You sure?'

'No probs - should be nice for us all to get together.'

The day came. Joseph was looking forward to seeing Ralph and the others. He wanted to be careful what he said, but maybe Ralph didn't fully understand what was happening to him. Just relax and enjoy it.

Jack picked him up at 12.30. Plenty of time to park and get in there before 1.00 p.m. He had not got round to speaking to Ralph. Hope he's ok. Alzheimer's. Why Ralph? Jack parked the car, and they both walked towards the entrance. Simon was already in the pub. He opened the door for them.

'Hi lads, how you doin'?'

'Not bad,' said Joseph, 'Ralph here?'

No one answered. Joseph walked into the pub. Jack ushered him towards the bar to get the first drinks. Just to the right of the bar an area they had reserved for the occasion. There must have been at least fifteen waiting for them.

'Come on Ralph, sit down,'

Joseph looked round, trying to spot his old friend Ralph.

'Come on mate, don't keep us waiting. We want to order the food.'

'How you doing Ralph?'

Joseph turned round. Everyone looking at him, sympathy pouring from their eyes.

'Jack, what's going on?'. Joseph felt a panic surge through him.

'Sit down mate, everyone's come here to see you. All your old friends.'

'But I'm Joseph.'

'Joseph died twenty years ago, Ralph. Don't worry, we understand. We'll look after you...'

Pigeon

He's there again. That middle-aged bloke at number thirty-six. Thinks he owns the place. I need to describe him so you can get an image of what a prat he is. Six feet, losing his hair from the front, glasses, and I imagine he used to be lanky. Spindly legs (God, I hope he doesn't wear **those** shorts this summer) but a ridiculous pot belly. Not sure if he's a drinker, just a bit pathetic in old age. Not the most attractive site first thing in the morning. I don't like him; neither do my mates. He's trying to get rid of us. Here we go again, the start of another day. Once again, the idiot's out to get me. Prat.

Here I am, minding my own business, sitting on the fence watching the world go by. I'll have a bit of a scratch – get rid of a few fleas. Those lice are a pest as well. Let's have a good go at them this morning. Bloody Hell, Prat's here again. Here he comes with his dawn chorus - clap, clap. Not sure he'd have the guts to actually hurt me, but I'll fly away anyway. There's always some bits and bobs to eat on the garage roof at number fifty-six in the next street. Best come back later.

Hang on, he's gone back in; just as well, I need to go to the loo. Nice and comfortable on his fence. He had the landscape gardeners in last month laying some nice expensive beige slabs. Soon sort that out. No, get in position, ready, aah... much better. Good, I've made a mess of his slabs. Serve him right, clapping his hands at me. Goes right through me, but I suppose that's the general idea. Reminds me, union meeting tonight. The lads have been moaning about Prat 'Ed and seem to blame me as it's my territory. Sorry lads, not my fault. I always get the brunt of it. Hang on, he's coming out again. Flippin' Eck, he's got a bucket of water; I'm off. Just hang about in that tree.

It's ok, he's spotted my doings. He likes a clean slab. Oh, get him, Fairy Liquid Deluxe (other washing-up liquids are available), scrubbing brush, the works. Still won't come off. His wife told him it's the berries we eat. Makes it a funny colour. You'll have to wait for a few days of rain. That'll shift it. Sure we have acid rain from Scandinavia these days. Shifts anything.

At least he hasn't got a cat. Or a dog. All things considered, I could be a lot worse off. He had foxes last year. He got rid of them, so we must give him some credit. I lost two of my mates to that fox. Never mind, the damn thing's gone now. If my patch was next door, food would be put out for me. Bits of biscuit, piece of bread, even those little blue pellets they accidently dropped in the soil around the plants. Not sure what they are. Bit exotic for my taste. Gave me a dicky tummy.

The main reason I don't like him is that he's ruining my love life. How can I bring a bird round when Old Prat Face keeps running out and clapping his hands? I wouldn't mind if it was a round of applause in appreciation of my performance, but it's like watching a folk singer on speed. Next thing you know he'll be putting his finger in one ear. After a bit of coo-cooing last Wednesday night, my last bird said she'd heard about the problems at my place and didn't believe it. She was prepared to give it a go, but never again. I don't mind being given the boot, but this is getting out of claw. He's got a lot to answer for. Don't know how his wife puts up with him. I'm getting desperate now, though. I'm the only one in the gang without a bird. Jim and Clive have produced three broods already this year. Jim says that 'er indoors is very pleased with their new gaff. I helped him with a few twigs the day they moved in. His missis gave me a funny look. Think she fancies me.

What's he up to now? The Prat's taking a cardboard box to the shed. Hang on, he's getting some tools out. Hammer, hacksaw, screwdriver. What's all this in aid of? I'll drop onto the shed roof for a closer look. What the... no one else knows that I can read. On the lid of the box it says 'Pigeon Spikes'. Now, unless he's entering me for the 400 meters relay I fear that Prat has gone and bought what is known as a 'Pigeon Deterrent'. Small (very sharp) plastic spikes are lined up in rows. You cut them to size and screw them to the top of the fence. Boy do they hurt your rear end. Old Tommy had to move house last year when his human occupant put them on every fence and on top of his shed. Tommy couldn't sit down for a week. Hang on, he's talking to the woman over the fence. Chatting her up? No, he's just warning them about the spikes.

'Let your husband know; just in case. It's seven foot to the top of the fence from your side, but you never know.'

'Think his climbing days are over.'

I know us pigeons only seem to sit and coo all day, but if we could talk, our level of humour and banter would be far more sophisticated. Wonder if he'll put them on the shed? My mates use that as the public loo. It goes down the back of the shed so he doesn't tend to notice. No, he's just doing the three fences overhanging his brand new slabs. Fair enough, I can live with that. I'll just do it over the lawn and the flower bed further down. As long as he leaves me alone. Hold up, here he comes.

'Get off, you stupid pigeon!'

More hand clapping.

Xen he is not. Think I'll nip round to Tommy's. See how he is. I'll share a curry with him and fly back home after. Make Prat's day.

I enjoyed that. Mind you, I couldn't wait until I'd got home, so I'll let him off today. What's he doing now? That neighbour's called him back. He's on the top of the ladder. Looks precarious. Even I think he should be careful.

Crikey, he's slipped forwards right on top of the fence. God that looks painful. Right through his trousers.

Someone should have warned him about the spikes...

Jenny of The Echo

I'll show them, she thought. Two weeks as a junior reporter and all they talk about is my legs. Jenny Greenhall was ambitious. The Banfield Echo, the local free paper, was a stepping stone to serious journalism. Aged twenty-six, with a degree in English, she attracted men in the office with her long, straight blond hair, slender but firm legs, and a figure a professional model would be proud of. Not interested in the hacks at the Echo, even young Bob, good looking and quiet; she was there for one reason – to progress to sub-editor within the year, editor within four years and then move to a bigger paper. The Echo was run by men, edited by a man, and any serious articles generally written by men. She was seen as the token female, something to adorn the office and who could be sent out to report on the local flower show.

Jeff Sneed, editor, seen as 'one of the lads', was prepared to give her a chance, but she had to work hard for it.

'No flower shows, beautiful baby competitions, eh?'

'That was just a figure of speech, Jeff, you know what I meant. I want the opportunity to take on the same stories as the men.'

'Ok, if that's what you want.   Get down to Jacobs and Sons, Bridge Street. Large builders' merchants.   We've had reports of clients being stitched up, refunds refused, that sort of thing.'

Jeff knew exactly what he was doing.   Simon Jacobs, the managing director of Jacobs and Sons, was a member at Jeff's golf club. He would do nothing to affect Simon's business, but he had to appear to be acting professionally.   She won't notice anything, he concluded.   If she found evidence that might hurt Jacobs, he'd edit the story to suit. No problem with an investigation as long as the public got the 'right' impression.   Jenny   arrived   at   Jacobs   and   felt uncomfortable within minutes. Four wolf whistles by the time she reached the trade counter.

'What can I do for you love?'

'Jenny Greenhall, Banfield Echo. Could I speak to Simon Jacobs please?'

Jacobs fancied himself and was in chat-up mode the moment she walked into his office.   Get your bloody eyes off me legs, she almost said aloud, glowering at him, and my chest come to that.

'We've had no complaints, one or two misunderstandings. I spoke to your boss, Jeff Sneed, only last week. He knows we've got nothing to answer for. If anyone's got a problem they should go to the police.'

She followed up with questions about customer complaints, returns policy, and the attitude of the staff at the trade counter.

'Look love, you're a pretty young thing. Do yourself a favour and trot off back to your office and make the tea or something. There's nothing for you here.'

'I will leave Mr Jacobs, but I don't appreciate being spoken to like that. If I find any malpractice here, I'll publish it and inform the authorities. Got it?'

'Keep your wig on love. You know where the door is, but if you'd like a drink sometime...'

She saw through Sneed's plan. Jacobs didn't care how many journalists paid a visit. An article would be tucked away on page five, next to the adverts for building and gardening materials, and Jacobs coming up smelling of roses. They were going through the motions. It was all lads together. One thing's for certain, she thought, I won't want be going for a drink with that slime ball.

Her next assignment was a particularly horrible court case. A woman in North Banfield had been repeatedly beaten by her husband after she tried to leave him, but this was before she met someone else. Her husband made the case that he was upset about her committing adultery and had reacted emotionally. Jenny had seen this type of case before, and she suspected the Echo would not want to report the case favourably from the point of view of the battered wife. Her suspicions were well founded, and although the husband was found guilty, Jeff once again edited the piece she submitted to the extent she didn't recognise it.

After a few assignments relating to betting shops, fishing competitions and arm wrestling bouts, Jenny was finally asked to report on something that Jeff knew she hated - football.

'Get down to Banfield Harriers for the next four matches, every other Saturday afternoon, just the home games. We want a full match analysis, pre and post interviews with the manager and captain.'

She didn't see the point in football. Twenty-two men kicking a piece of leather around a field, trying to get it between the posts. The crowds are tribal, abusive, and again, male dominated. However, for the first time, some of the men at the office were jealous. For the first time, she had an assignment they wanted. This didn't help the atmosphere at work, but she took this as an opportunity to break through into a male bastion.

The first match, against Bromsgrove Rovers, was a dull affair. One good goal, she reckoned, giving The Banners a slender victory. Corner from the right by Keith Jones, whipped in low, deflection, and slammed into the top corner by the marauding captain, Chris Batson.

'Chris, you're out of the bottom three with that victory. Where do you go from here?'

'Come and watch us every week, Jenny, we can only improve. Tell your readers we've got big plans at The Banners. We signing two new players next week.'

For the first time, she was being treated with respect. As the weeks went by, the game she had viewed as pointless began to take hold. The tactics, the team camaraderie, physical effort, and no little skill. Her fortnightly reports began to get noticed. People wrote to Jenny of the Echo with comments for her back page reports. Jeff wanted to see her, first thing Monday morning.

'We're taking you off the football. Colin's stepping in; think we need a change of direction.'

'You can't do that; I'm just getting going.'

'Listen. I'm editor; I say who does what around here.'

'I may be a girl, but I'm a good reporter. Think I've found my niche.'

'Don't need any fancy words from you. Now, take your niche off to the book festival in Kinver village. More your sort of thing.'

There was no arguing with him, so Colin Wexford reported on the next few Banfield home games. The complaints started to come in. Readers wanted her back, the manager of the football club even chipped in.

'Don't know what's happened Jeff, but that girl is good. For your own sake, drop Wexford and bring her back in.'

Further comments from advertisers gave Jeff no choice. She was back at the football. For the rest of the season she submitted reports that any top sports journalist would have been proud to write. Then, she had the surprise of her life when Jeff called her into his office.

'We're had a call from the Midland Football Writers' Association. You've been nominated for an award. You're guaranteed at least top three, and the Echo has been invited to Molineux for a presentation dinner. Four of us are going, and you're with us.'

'I don't know what to say.'

'Listen Jen, I think I treated you badly when you first started. I'm sorry, really sorry. You're a good kid, a brilliant writer, and as good as any of the blokes here. You've nailed it as far as football is concerned.'

The Chairman of Wolverhampton Wanderers introduced the candidates for the various awards. The one they were waiting for - Best New Football Reporter – was next.

'We've followed the progress of a new, young reporter with great interest this season. I have great pleasure in announcing the winner - the Best Football Reporter for 2015 is...'

She drew breath; third place would be ok. Wonder if he meant the 'best' football reporter or the 'best new' reporter? It seemed an age as her mind worked overtime, hoping...

'Jenny Greenhall, Banfield Echo.'

The room exploded with applause. Jeff kissed her on the cheek, and as she rose to collect the award, a nod of acceptance from Colin Wexford and a smile from Bob.

'You're ok Jenny. You've made it.'

'Thanks Bob, maybe we could celebrate with a drink later.'

'That would be nice. Word of warning, keep your distance from the boss. He's always after a new conquest. I don't want to see you get hurt.'

'No danger of that.'

After her success at the football writers' awards, she followed Bob's advice (not that she needed it), and concentrated on football. Over the next two years she developed a reputation as one of the best sports writers in the Midlands. By that time, Jeff Sneed had moved on, Bob became the new editor, and the whole ethos of the paper changed – for the better. Jenny is now senior sports editor for a national newspaper and makes regular appearances on local radio. She had won the battle against sexism in her place of work and became a complete convert over to the sport she previously thought was a waste of time.

She Blames Me

She's there again today. A tall, thin woman; probably in her twenties. An old-fashioned hairstyle, like they used to have during the war, and she's wearing a long thick overcoat with large lapels. A dark blue scarf is wrapped around her neck. Not a cold day, and it appears strange to be wrapped up in such a way. I've seen her a few times, and she's looking in my direction. Sitting on the seat nearest the rear platform by the exit door, she can survey all the passengers, but she's only looking at me. I can't see her face clearly; she has the hood pulled up. No one else seems to notice her.

This time she follows me. On previous occasions, she stayed on the bus as I got off and I sensed that her eyes latched onto mine. She turned her head towards me as I looked through the window. I looked back. No one else did. This time I begin to feel nervous. She's keeping at least twenty yards behind me.

'Hi John,' a neighbour greets me as I reach the front gate.

I turn round; she's gone.

The next day, it happens again. The nights are drawing in, and I'm late tonight. Street lights are on and no one else in the street. As I open the front gate I look round. She stops. I need to get into the house, fumbling with the keys. Look through the front window. She's standing there, by the lamppost.

This continues for a few weeks, and then one night I get really scared. I pull the curtains back slightly, just enough to get a view of the street. One street light within five yards of my front garden. She is standing there, and as I look in her direction, she raises her head. I still can't see her eyes, but again sense that I am the target. She raises her hand and points; first towards me, then towards the roof of the house. Is she trying to tell me something?

A week before Christmas. I've lived on my own for ten years, and Christmas is the only time that loneliness creeps into my thoughts and emotions. No family now, and a visit or call from friends, neighbours or work colleagues would be very welcome. A knock at the window. Doorbell not working? Pulling the curtains to one side, I draw breath when she appears there. My heart is racing, I feel dizzy. She points at me again, then turns to look towards the roof of the house and points in that direction.

'What do you want?' I cry out.

Panic has set in, and I feel ashamed and look again; she's no longer there. Every time it happens, she's getting closer and closer. I jump with fright as the phone rings. No one there.

I have to control this, can't let it rule my life. It occurred to me that she is pointing to the eaves of the house. The attic? Is there something upstairs that she wants me to know about? With some trepidation, switching on all the lights, I climb the stairs to the top floor, a room I hardly use. These old Victorian houses have attics rather than lofts. At least there's no need to climb a ladder. I dumped a few boxes in the attic when I moved in ten years ago. Other than that, a couple of old trunks lie in the corner. Never thought to look at them before. Try the first one. Christmas cards, old books, theatre programmes. I open the other one. A single item, an old Radio Times folder, leather-bound, sits at the bottom of the trunk. I shudder as the air goes cold around me. I must open the folder. Taking it out of the trunk is an effort – not a physical effort, but I sense the answer is close.

As I open the folder, a pile of newspaper cuttings fall out and a gust of air blows them across the attic floor. Trying to collect them up, one cutting stands out, draws me in. I'm on my knees, ignoring the cobwebs and dust. The article in front of me; dated December 1937. 'Young woman strangled on Christmas Eve'. The article describes how Barbara Smithson travelled on the no. 26 bus from the centre of town every night on her way home. She lived in this house. Someone she worked with had pestered her for months. In those days, women rarely complained. He followed her home and she refused his advances. He pushed her into the house and there was a struggle. He told the court how she slapped his face, kicked him, screaming at him, pleading for him to leave. He lost his temper. She kicked him again and tried to push him away. He had his hands round her throat. Pressing down hard, she stopped breathing. His finger-marks clear, purple marks on her slim neck. The blue scarf she wore was buried with her. He went to the gallows, strung up for taking a young innocent life.

Christmas Eve. I'm sitting in the dim light of the front room. Curtains closed, a few ancient lights on the tree with a dull glow spreading across the room. She's here, the room goes cold. As she appears in the room, her face is still covered by the hood of her coat, but I can see the outline of her chin, and a faint glow that frightens me. She slowly pulls back the hood and her eyes bore into me. Eyes red with flame, it is though they are scanning my soul, deep within me. Her hand moves towards the scarf and she takes it away from her neck. She glares at me as I see the purple marks, fingerprints that had taken her life. She points at me and opens her mouth to speak, but there is just a gasp. She cannot speak.

'It wasn't me,' I say in a weak voice.

'You died in 1937. It was someone else who took your life. He hung for his crime and he's gone to hell for what he did. Please believe me.'

A pause, and she lowers her hand. As if in recognition of my plea, she takes a step back and once again places the hood over her head. The glow of her eyes becomes dim. I feel faint, and she is retreating.

She is gone.

Printed in Great Britain
by Amazon.co.uk, Ltd.,
Marston Gate.